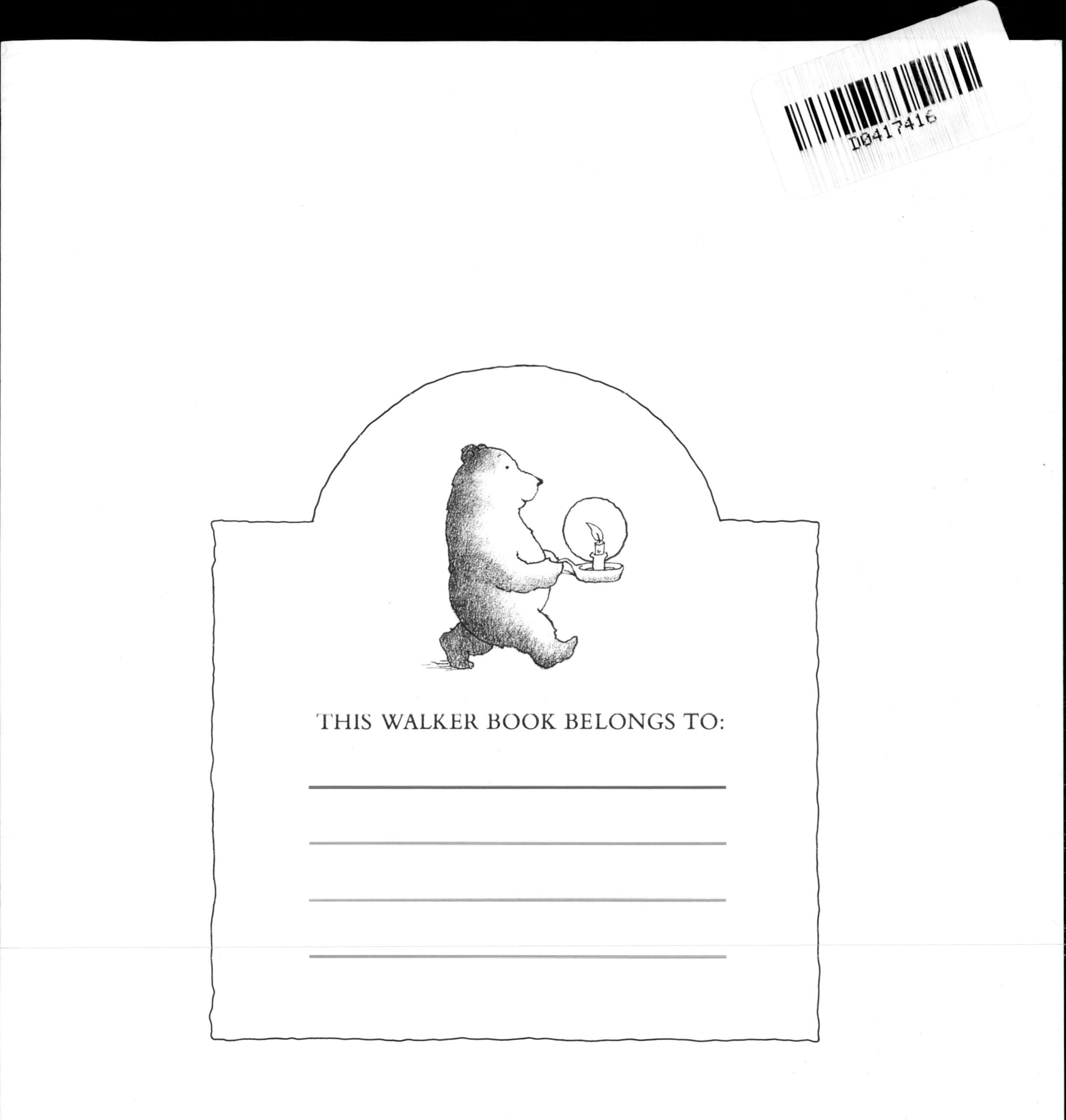
THIS WALKER BOOK BELONGS TO:

The Magic Bicycle

Written by
BRIAN PATTEN

Illustrated by
ARTHUR ROBINS

WALKER BOOKS
AND SUBSIDIARIES
LONDON • BOSTON • SYDNEY

Adapted from Brian Patten's poem, "The Saga of the Doomed Cyclist", which first appeared in *Gargling with Jelly*, published by Viking Kestrel in 1985. First published 1993 by Walker Books Ltd, 87 Vauxhall Walk, London SE11 5HJ. This edition published 1995. This Book has been typeset in Berkeley. Printed in Hong Kong. British Library Cataloguing in Publication Data. A catalogue record for this book is available from the British Library. ISBN 0-7445-3651-0. 10 9 8 7 6 5 4

When Danny Harris knocked a witch
Into a muddy roadside ditch
She put a spell on his bike:

"Like it or lump it, lump it or like,

Ride on forever, little tike!"

The pedals hissed, the bike frame glowed,
The tyres clung to the lonely road.
The bike was magic, it came alive,
And Danny's legs went into overdrive.

When Danny set off for Timbuktu
He found Ben Nevis blocked his view.
He puffed and panted to the top
And even then he could not stop.

Like it or lump it, lump it or like,
He was glued by magic to the magic bike!

Passing through London on his way to Dover
He knocked a policeman and a guardsman over.

His back was aching,
His legs felt dead,
He wanted to crawl
Back home to bed.

Instead he cycled through the Chunnel
and he spent an hour
Whizzing around the Eiffel Tower.

When he crossed the snowcapped Pyrenees
The frost and the sunlight burnt his knees.

In Spain his magic bicycle coasted
On to the beach where sunbathers roasted.

He finally fulfilled a lifelong wish
As the bike drifted down among the fish.

"The floor of the Mediterranean Sea is a very strange place for a boy to be."

In Tangier he found a bazaar full of spices
(He'd rather have found some bizarre lolly ices).

In the African desert Danny went
Crashing into a Bedouin's tent.

By the time Mount Kilimanjaro came into view
He'd been bitten by scorpions and snakes
(and a camel too).

He swung up through Egypt and crossed the Nile
On the back of a sleepy crocodile.

He cycled through Kuwait, Iraq and Iran,
And into the mountains of Afghanistan.

He rode through Russia where the biggest hurdle
Was navigating the Arctic Circle.
His wheels were frozen. He spent several nights
Sliding under the Northern Lights.

He was up to his neck in frozen snow
By the time he got to Ontario.

He thought he was lost,
His bike was a wreck
By the time he had made it
Through Quebec.

Near Niagara Falls the bike took pity
And it flew him down to New York City.

BEST
FLY
BRUSH
ROOMS
HOTEL
BIG BURGER
FIZZ
BAR
BEER
HAVE A NICE DAY
FOOD
COCKTAILS
Music
MOVIES
PIZZA
EATS
RESTAURANT
BAR
DISCO
ICE CREAM
ALL YOU CAN EAT
15¢
TAXI
I ♥ NY

At night Times Square was the colour of sweets –
A gigantic neon-lit bag of treats.

Down at the docks on the stroke of midnight
A ghostly ship sailed into sight.
It was manned by a frightful skeleton crew
Who whispered, "We're homeward bound – you come too."

14

Onto the deck the battered bike drifted,
Its wheels were buckled, its frame was twisted.
Flying fish and seagulls made salty jokes,
Octopuses were tangled in its spokes.

Danny cycled in his sleep,
He was weary and frantic.
Round and round the deck he went
As they crossed the Atlantic.

He dreamt that mermaids and scarecrows danced on an ice floe,
And the boat sailed on through oceanic snow.

He arrived in Liverpool and once ashore
Bumped into the same witch as he had before.
She snarled, "I'm in a hurry, I want that bike!"
And Danny smiled, "Keep it as long as you like."

She climbed on the bike, forgetting her curse,

And rode forever

through the *Universe*.

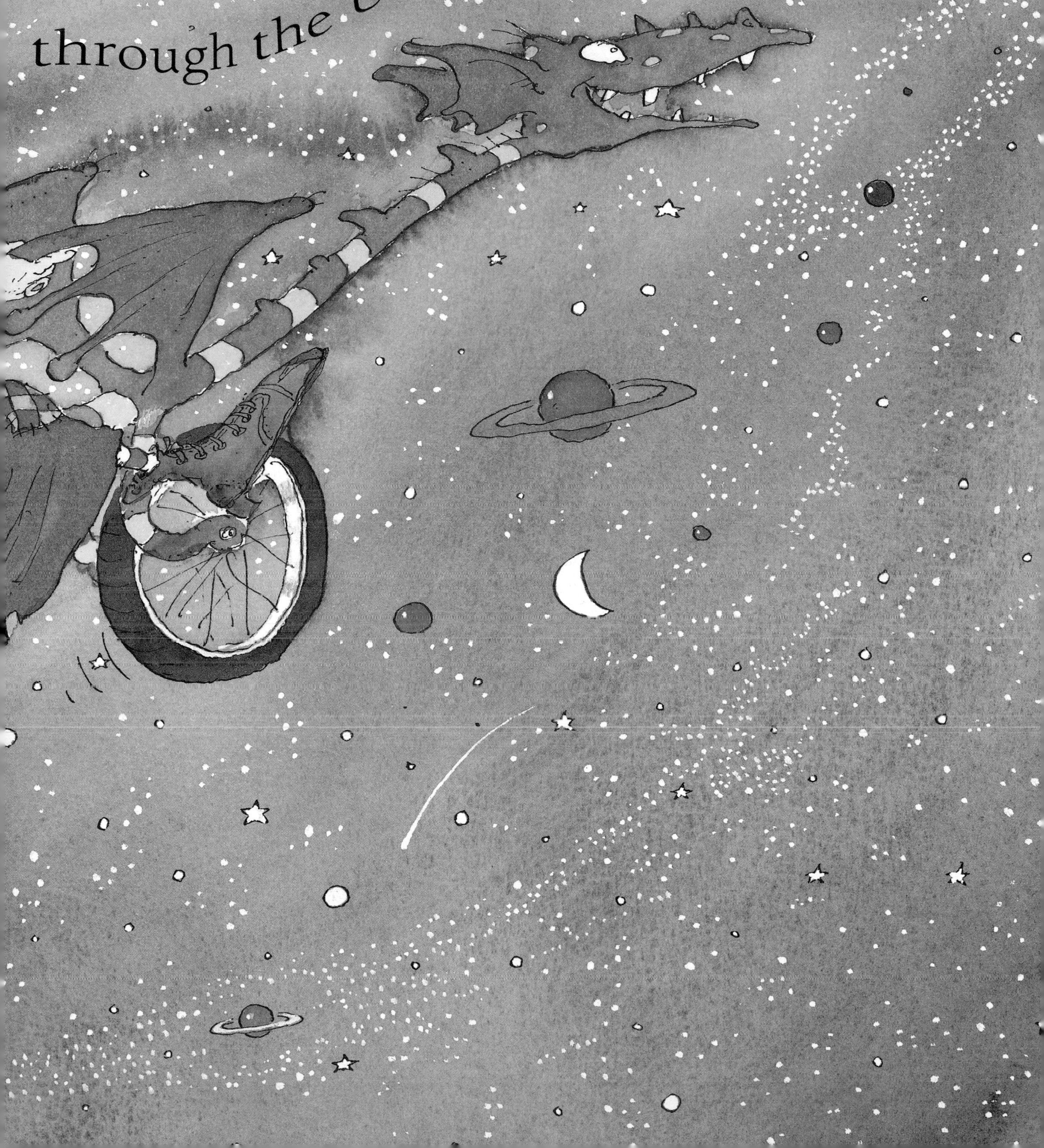